Sept 1982

My dear wonderful Rachel,

I am so lucky to have you as my ~~niece~~.

I love you ~~more~~ than the whole wide world.

love,

Aunt Barbara

Pajama Walking

Story by Vicki Kimmel Artis
Pictures by Emily Arnold McCully

Houghton Mifflin Company   Boston   1981

Library of Congress Cataloging in Publication Data
Artis, Vicki Kimmel.
    Pajama walking.
    SUMMARY: When Bessie stays overnight at Clara's
house, their fun includes a bedroom picnic and choco-
late toothpaste.
    [1. Night—Fiction] I. McCully, Emily Arnold.
II. Title.
PZ7.A7473Paj   [E]   80-22658
ISBN 0-395-30343-5

Text Copyright © 1981 by Vicki Kimmel Artis

Illustrations copyright © 1981 by Emily Arnold McCully

Printed in the United States of America

Y 10 9 8 7 6 5 4 3 2 1

Especially for my dad and mom,
Bob and Clara,
and for Gregory, Tad, and Shane

V.K.A.

Pajama Walking

Bedroom Picnic

Bessie was staying at Clara's house for the night.

Clara said, "It would be fun to have a picnic. Let's eat in my bedroom."

Mom gave them dinner and a tablecloth.

Clara and Bessie ran upstairs and set out their picnic dinner.

"Something's missing," said Clara. "There aren't enough friends at our picnic. Let's invite Turtle."

Bessie put some salad on the tablecloth.

Clara put Turtle on the lettuce.

"Now let's invite my ants," she said.

Bessie put a french fry on the tablecloth.

Clara put ants from her ant farm on the french fry.

"We still need more friends," said Clara. "Let's invite my cat."

Bessie put a piece of hamburger on the tablecloth.

Clara came back with Muggins the cat.

"This is great," said Clara.

But Bessie was not so sure. "The ants must not like french fries," she said. "They left."

Clara and Bessie searched.

"Mom will be mad if I don't find them," said Clara. "We'll have to trap them on something sticky."

Clara ran downstairs and got the honey jar.

They spread honey on a napkin and put it on the floor.

"In the morning we'll take the ants out of the honey and put them back in the ant farm," said Clara. "Then Mom won't be mad."

"Now where's Turtle?" asked Bessie.

Turtle was gone.

Clara looked under the bed.

Bessie picked up her pajamas.

"Clara! Yuk, it's Turtle. It's Turtle. He's crawling on my pajamas. Get him off. Get him off."

Clara pulled Turtle out of Bessie's pajamas.

"Turtle's very clean," said Clara.

She put him back in his bowl.

Clara and Bessie returned to their picnic.

"Look at Muggins," said Clara.

The cat had stepped on the honey paper.

He looked up at Clara.

His ears flattened back.

He shook his paw and rolled on Bessie's dinner plate.

Clara picked up the cat and pulled the paper off
his legs.

She put Muggins out in the hall and closed the door.

There were honey spots on the floor.

"We'll clean this up after the ants come back," explained
Clara. "It's okay, Bessie. We can still have our picnic. We'll
share."

"But there are no friends at our picnic," said Bessie.

"Yes there are," said Clara. "Two best friends."

Toenails

Clara and Bessie sat on the bathroom floor.

Clara asked, "Do you want nail polish on your toenails?"

"No, I don't," said Bessie.

"Why not?" asked Clara. "Grownups wear nail polish."

"My mom doesn't," said Bessie. "She thinks it looks terrible."

Clara pouted.

"My mom looks beautiful with nail polish on," Clara said. "I'm going to use some. I'm big now. When I was little I did silly things."

"What did you do?" asked Bessie.

Clara thought.

"I ran into the kitchen and said, 'My'm a big deer!'
Then I danced around like a deer. That was when I was
little."

"That was when you were silly," said Bessie. "When I
was little, I drew pictures in the dark to see if I could get
the eyes in the right place."

"I was a horse on Halloween once."

"I was a witch."

"I'm glad I'm grown up now," said Clara. "Now I don't do dumb things. When I was little, I was silly."

Clara took off her shoes and socks.

"Don't you want to paint your toenails? They'll look beautiful."

"No," said Bessie. "I'm going to try lipstick."

"I tried lipstick before," bragged Clara. "Pass the nail polish."

"What color?" Bessie asked. "Red or orange?"

"Both," said Clara. "I'll paint my big toes red and my little toes orange."

"That will be beautiful," said Bessie. "Do all grownups paint their toes like that?"

"Only some of them," said Clara.

"Which ones?" asked Bessie.

"The girls," said Clara.

Chocolate Toothpaste

Clara and Bessie brushed their teeth.

"This toothpaste is too strong," said Bessie. "I wish it was chocolate."

"Chocolate would be the best," agreed Clara.

She made a terrible face.

She spit out the toothpaste.

"We could make chocolate toothpaste," she said.

Clara ran to the kitchen and came back with a bag of chocolate chips.

Bessie got the toothpaste.

The chocolate was too big to fit in the tube.

Clara squeezed the toothpaste into a bowl.

Bessie added the chips.

They mashed the chocolate with two forks.

"It looks chunky," said Bessie.

"We should test it," said Clara.

Clara got chocolate on her lips.

Bessie's teeth turned brown.

"Delicious," said Clara. She spit out every bit.

"Delicious," agreed Bessie, trying not to make a sour face.

Clara took the toothpaste into the kitchen and came back with a bowl of strawberries.

They ate until the terrible toothpaste taste went away.

They ate until only berry juice was left.

"Look," said Clara. "War paint."

She put her finger in the juice and drew lines on Bessie's face.

Then she painted her own face.

Bessie laughed.

Clara laughed.

Mom walked in.

"What's going on here?" she asked.

Bessie said, "We were inventing chocolate toothpaste."

Mom looked at Clara's painted face.

"What's this?" she asked.

"Indian war paint," said Bessie.

"Strawberry juice," confessed Clara.

Mom kissed Clara's cheek.

"I think you've invented a way to make kisses taste better," she said. "Where is your chocolate toothpaste?"

Bessie and Clara looked for the bowl.
They couldn't find it.
Mom asked, "Did it have chocolate chips?"
"Lots of them," said Clara.
Mom said, "Your dad thought it was his sundae."
"Stop him!" cried Bessie.
Then they heard a yell.
Bessie covered her eyes.
Clara covered her mouth.
"Too late," said Mom.

Pajama Walking

It was bedtime and the house was quiet.

"It's dark in here," whispered Bessie.

"Don't think about it," Clara said.

"I'm scared," said Bessie.

She hid under the blankets.

"I can fix that," bragged Clara. "We can play games so you won't think of the dark."

Clara bounced out of bed and ran out the door.

"Don't leave me," cried Bessie.

But Clara was gone.

"It's dark, it's dark, and the monsters are here," Bessie wailed.

Clara came back with Dad's pajamas.

"I'm not a monster, I'm just Clara," she said. "Let's pajama walk."

Clara put on Dad's giant pajamas.

"Now you get in with me."

Bessie sat on Clara's lap and put her legs in the pajama legs and her arms in the pajama arms.

There were two people in one pair of pajamas.

"Now we grab the bed and stand up," Clara said.

She grabbed with her right hand, but Bessie grabbed with her left.

They fell over and rolled into the wall.

Bessie giggled.

They held onto the table and pulled themselves up.

"I can do it. I can walk," said Clara.

She stepped with her right foot, but Bessie stepped with her left.

They fell over and rolled into the hallway.

"This is hard work," Clara said. "I need milk. It's downstairs."

They stood up and marched to the steps.

"I can't get down there," said Bessie.

"Sure you can," said Clara.

She stepped down too soon.

Bessie stepped back.

Clara stepped up.

Bessie stepped down.

They grabbed the railing and slid down the stairs on Clara's back.

"My tongue's drying out," said Clara.

"Shhhhhhhh."

Bessie giggled.

She helped Clara stand up, and they walked carefully to the kitchen.

Then they poured a glass of milk, and Bessie watched Clara drink.

Her hand hung near Clara's nose.

Bessie tickled the nose a little.

Clara snickered.

Bessie tickled a little more.

Clara sputtered milk down her chin.

"You sound like a washing machine," whispered Bessie.

Clara laughed and sputtered the milk all around.

"I can clean this up tomorrow," she said as she looked at the mess. "Let's have a circus. Let's do a somersault."

"Don't," begged Bessie, but it was too late.

Clara dove.

Bessie fell over.

Her face disappeared down the front of the pajamas.

Her head bumped on Clara's stomach and she laughed.

Then the light flashed on.

"Did I hear noise?" asked Dad.

"Noooooooo," said Clara.

"Nooooooo," said Bessie.

"I must have dreamed all that bumping," said Dad. "It's very late."

Bessie and Clara tried to stand up.

They fell over and rolled under the table.

"Am I dreaming all this giggling?" asked Dad.

"Yessssssss," said Bessie.

"Yesssssssss," said Clara.

"Upstairs," said Dad.

They tried to climb the steps, but Bessie fell on her hands and knees.

Clara flopped on Bessie's back like a turtle shell.

"Now," said Dad.

Clara unbuttoned the pajamas, and Bessie rolled out on the floor.

Dad led them up the steps to their room.

Bessie sat on the bed and said, "It's too dark, Clara. I try to act big but then I get scared again."

Clara answered, "I know what will take your mind off the dark."

She opened the door and turned on the hall light.

"That will take your mind off the dark," explained Clara.

She got into bed.

"I'm not sleepy," she said. "I think I'll just rest."

"I think I'll rest too," agreed Bessie.

"You don't mind if I snore while I rest, do you?" asked Clara.

"No," answered Bessie. "I think I can snore now too."

Clara rolled over.

Bessie said, "You pulled the blankets off. Now my back is all bare."

"All bear," yawned Clara. "I thought it was all human."

Bessie sputtered.

Clara sputtered.

And they giggled themselves to sleep.